I0538608

SINS OF THE SAVIORS

PREQUEL:

THE NETWORK APOSTATE

TJ Relk

Copyright © 2024 by TJ Relk

All rights reserved.

No part of this publication may be reproduced, distributed, or transmitted in any form or by any means, including photocopying, recording, or other electronic or mechanical methods, without the prior written permission of the publisher, except as permitted by U.S. copyright law.

For more information about the Sins of the Saviors series, to contact the author, or to obtain permission requests, contact Dystopian Dreams Press at: dystopiandreamspress@outlook.com .

The story, all names, characters, and incidents portrayed in this production are fictitious.

Book Cover by Miblart

First edition: 2024

ISBN: 979-8-9920471-3-4

Entries

"If everybody always lies to you, the consequence is not that you believe the lies,
but rather that nobody believes anything any longer. ...
And with such a people you can then do what you please."

Hannah Arendt, German philosopher

June 21

I once feared no one took my warnings seriously. Now I fear someone might. So, I say nothing.

I do not know the whole truth. Moreover, I have not the slightest clue what I would ask others to do if I ever put together its scattered pieces. All I know for certain is that we have been lied to about the forever war.

The fragments I have are not enough to alarm people. I will not put my shrinking circle of family and friends at risk. When I have enough information, I will reveal it. For now, I write this journal to remind myself what the truth looks like, to keep from sliding under the warm blanket of lies part of me wants so desperately to embrace.

No one much cared when we protested the years of deceptions, the slow trickle of small lies that culminated in the wholesale rewriting of history. Many of those old enough to remember the time before the war recognized what was going on and failed to call it out. Network enablers, then as now, are richly rewarded for playing along. I hate their endless compromises and hate myself for sometimes being in their ranks.

Our people have changed. We have become used to being lied to. A constant barrage of Goliath Network infotainment and trivialities gradually discredited truth as an antiquated and relative construct. The new citizen mindscape considered truth little and valued it even less.

But I'm talking about exposing the Goliath Network itself, not debunking any score of its individual fictions—attacking the hive instead of swatting at bees in an angry swarm. This is about the game itself, not merely the actions on the field.

This should be different. People should listen. People should care. A lie big enough to wake the masses. That is the hope.

I am Jane Veristo. I will document my research in this journal. I'll be the proselytizer of truth I should have always been. I will find it and spread it and be at peace for the effort.

If fools pick the beautiful lie instead of the ugly truth, I cannot be responsible. I assume it to be ugly. Otherwise, why lie about it?

June 22

Collecting evidence has become my hidden purpose. I've amassed quite a stash. A point of pride I can share with no one.

I only see random snippets of a larger picture hidden behind the firewall. I yearn to see it all, but, in moments of honest self-reflection, I wonder if I'd be capable of recognizing it. I doubt my atrophied brain could comprehend what must be an unimaginably complex, three-dimensional canvas of deception.

There's an urgency to fill the holes in that canvas. I can't assume what I've uncovered will go unnoticed or ignored forever. I can't wait for the perfect, iron-clad case. If it leads where I think it leads, Goliath will react, and this journal will abruptly end.

I hear rumors that private space laws will be rescinded at the end of the year. It scares the hell out of me. If it happens, the Network will have total, 24/7 access to me. Awake, asleep, in the bathroom—whenever and wherever. Goliath will tear back the curtains to my apartment refuge to peer into my subversive soul.

Where will I practice my memory? Where will I stow and study new evidence? Where will I be myself?

I won't have the luxury of time forever. If I'm going to make a stand, it has to be soon. So, I will start laying out the breadcrumbs in this journal. Perhaps a mapping of my evidence to date will help me identify the gaps, revealing the bigger lie.

I start with my brother's death. I might have ignored the contradictions I found, as I ignored countless lesser incongruities. But these lies were painfully personal.

It's been eleven years, but the day is still seared in my memory. I can replay it frame by frame. Not that I need to. No one does. Next of kin ceremonies are recorded, so anyone can download it in razor-sharp detail from infinite angles. Network memory is as comprehensive as it is flawless. It is always preferred to personal recollections.

The Network's main feed starts with a wide, aerial shot of my parent's front yard as the military motorcade pulls up behind a small, raised stage set up next to the road. My family is sitting in the front row of a couple dozen chairs on our fake turf.

My dad hated that turf, but replanting grass was still years away. We were recovering from the worst years of the warming. Even in a relatively cool mountain valley, it was 102 degrees this November 10th.

The military wouldn't confirm whether it was a promotion, award, or next-of-kin ceremony. This was intentional. Event producers strove to capture short public attention spans with genuine expressions of pride or grief when the event intent was revealed. Viewers were drawn in by the suspense, a patriotic ruse to maximize pro-war messaging.

Goliath broadcasts such events in regional media markets to drive home the war's impact to family, friends, and neighbors. In our area, local-impact stories were distributed throughout the eight small towns in our rural valley.

After the wide shot, the video zooms in on my mother. She fans herself nervously in the heat, staring a thousand yards past the stage as she waits to find out what kind of war hero her son will be—living or dead. We had not heard from David for almost 20 years.

My dad takes her hand, trying to comfort her. My mom waves him off to maintain a stoic demeanor for the cameras. A sharply uniformed soldier unfurls a flag taken from the lead vehicle. He marches it up some stairs to the front of the stage between a formation of ten ceremonial soldiers, five on each side. They fire their antique M1 rifles in unison after he passes through them. He places the flag in a stand behind the podium, takes his place at the head of the formation, and marches the pretend soldiers offstage.

A suited lady emerges from a small gaggle of officials gathered at the side of the stage. She takes the podium and launches into her speech. She tries to be dramatic, but speeches this well-rehearsed and oft-heard drain passion from both givers and receivers.

She begins, "It is with great sadness..."

Instantly, we know David is dead. The rest of the speech becomes so much background noise to our grief, a checklist for the fallen:

- David died honorably serving his country, defending our people.

- One of many. Not the first or the last.

- A reminder of the sacrifice we need to honor, the order we must defend, the war we must continue to feed with soldiers like David.

The formal ceremony is over in minutes, culminating with the delivery of remains to my parents. My dad rises to accept the wooden urn. My mom can't muster the strength. She has become a blubbering, weeping husk of a woman. My sister,

Mary, drapes a comforting arm over her as both look at the ground, waiting for the event to pass.

Local dignitaries jockey for a word with the bereaved for as long as the Network media crew lingers. When they leave, the crowds vanish. The combination of next-of-kin notification, funeral, and local war rally ends as abruptly as it began. Staging is disassembled inside of fifteen minutes. Our small family is left standing in the middle of the empty yard in awkward silence. Without the cameras, we don't know what to do.

David is instantly forgotten, as are most things by most people. Memory is an unnecessary burden. Only David's closest family and friends will remember him now. All will rely on the ceremony video as the event's true record. An eternal tribute from a grateful nation. A digital tombstone.

You won't see me in the video. I was there, seated next to my sister. I reacted with more disbelief than grief. I shook my fist a few times during the speech and wanted to flip off the Defense Department speaker, but I don't remember if I followed through. Probably. Not what they were going for, regardless, so they edited me out.

The Goliath Network paints the visual narrative. It exploits our misplaced belief in what we see. It uses our eyes against us.

It was hard enough being cut out of David's "sacrifice ceremony"—their buzzword for funerals of fallen soldiers. Then they docked me social merit points for not performing to their expectations. When I complained, they told me I was mistaken and took away more points. That put me below the threshold for my office job, and I was reassigned to landscaping. I lost my house and was assigned a small apartment. I stopped complaining.

Merit points are the exclusive currency now. Unfortunately, you can't cash out your Merit Indicator when it's high, like we used to do with stocks and bonds. Nor does it hold some static value, like the physical cash we mostly stopped using when I was a kid.

Goods and services are purchased not in exchange for anything you own but based on the Network's valuation of you. That value changes continually—every second of every day until you're dead. As the Network puts it, "Do good today. Do good tomorrow. Every day counts."

You can't have an off day. As Mary advises me, "Fake it till you make it." She has blissfully lost all track of the border between her internal, genuine self and her external, phony self.

To this day, most of my family thinks I skipped David's ceremony, even those who attended the event. All of this was designed to dissuade me, to tame me, to tempt me with the advantages you only get by embracing the lies, large and small, that make United America work.

I continued searching for holes in the official story. I ran an analysis on a sample of my brother's remains. Not David's ashes, it turned out, or anyone else's.

My family cried over a wooden box filled with wood ash. As I researched the battle David supposedly died in, I found more "alternative facts"—what we used to call lies. I was furious.

I shared these discoveries with no one. Some of this was cowardice, I suppose, but I was no longer willing to be a martyr for a cause only I believed in.

Before David's "death," I had quieted my once-loud political and social criticisms to the occasional muttered growl, mostly to myself. I will remain silent until I can make a case strong enough to convince the most ardent Network believer. I will be patient.

June 23

The evidence will make more sense if I present it in sequence. The next tranche needs to be accurately documented. I have not seen it in years and need to retrieve it. That's a trip that can't happen until next weekend.

I don't keep anything too damning in the apartment. Cameras are pretty much everywhere. It's going to take a whole day to get to the place I buried it. ICom tracks me, but it should look like I'm taking a hike in the woods, consistent with my preferences and patterns.

Until then, I'll try to explain how I got to this point. If this journal is to be believed, I need to be honest about my intentions. As honest as I can be.

Long before my brother's supposed death, I was a critic of the new government and its all-encompassing Goliath Network. I paid a price.

But it is also true that I waited too long. I was busy and self-occupied. I waited for others to push back against the tides that so thoroughly debased this place and possessed its people. Tides that washed away our concern about truth, sacrifice, each other. Tides that gradually revealed our true nature of fear, self-interest, and lethargy. A darkness celebrated as virtue.

I tried frantically to fight the unrelenting currents, to pull back the lost sands of who we were back to dry land. It left me exhausted and empty, a target and an outcast. I became a time fugitive, trapped in echoes of a world only I seemed to hear.

My friends and family did not understand this devotion to an idealized past that they insist I've romanticized and embellished. They pleaded for me to let this new world of entertainment, convenience, and desires wash over me, or at least to let them bask in it in peace.

After years of thankless struggle against the creeping dominance of Goliath, I began to succumb. I realized I was only fighting against my own happiness. I criticized less, thought less, cared less. As I relented, my social merit score increased and new opportunities were opened to me, new pleasures accessible.

By the time David "died," we had all embraced the new order or become quiet collaborators. The specter of my brother reminded me who I once was. Who I should be again.

I was closer to David than anyone else in the family. I missed that kind kid who overthought everything and would come to me for advice about homework, or girls, or whatever. David always stood up for me. He'd routinely cover for my chores when I snuck out to parties. I remember he picked me up in the middle of the night after I got in a fight with a boyfriend, even though he was years away from having a driver's license.

I missed David. I wondered what kind of man he'd turn into. Now, I didn't even know if he was alive.

I continue quietly building my case, alone and away from Network tracking—a compromise between conviction and self-preservation. Conspiring against a system so woven into our lives, thoughts, and bodies is daunting. My fear of it keeps me careful.

It keeps me from speaking freely. It keeps me from openly meeting up with other Goliath critics, beyond my group of book exchange eccentrics. It keeps me from accepting a cryptic invitation tucked into one of my forbidden books. Even with well-known friends and neighbors, I never loan out that book.

June 24

Generations have passed. I can't assume anyone who reads this will know the context. There are endless droves of Network data about the war and the transition, of course. But the official history has received so many facelifts that it's unrecognizable to anyone who lived through it.

Most skeptics—when we had skeptics—would tell you the turning point was the day the war was declared. It is now known as Patriotic Unity Day or simply Patriots Day. There's no record of it now, but, at the time, most people called it transition day.

A fever panic swept the nation, fed by a constant barrage of horror stories that started with attacks on Europe and Taiwan by unimaginable regional alliances. Our enemies' nonnegotiable goal: our complete destruction by any means. The revolting footage of children mowed down, women tortured, and hostages taken could not be denied; it proved the brutal savagery of a subhuman enemy. A wave of attacks followed on our troops, embassies, and citizens abroad.

We saw it with our own eyes. We were attacked. We were losing.

By morning, the war was no longer a distant, overseas affair. Every hour, we were pelted with new reports of possible homeland attacks: cyber, banking, biological. Sleeper agents were said to be targeting statehouses, schools, and hospitals, with terrorist reinforcements flooding across the poorly guarded border.

After a day of frantic, unconfirmed reports about existential threats, President Wolfe addressed the country. I was in the car. Like everyone else, I pulled over to listen. I'd barely parked when he started, "My fellow Americans..."

The familiar refrain instantly put me at ease. I waited for a calm assessment of what was real and what was rumor, a reassurance of our strength and resolve, a call for unity. But it was a perfunctory introduction, and calm was not his intent.

Following a long, dramatic pause looking down at his desk, President Wolfe stared back into us through the camera. "We've been through a lot the last 24 hours. It's worse than you think. You're afraid. You should be."

His voice gradually rose to a crescendo. "I'm not just talking about foreign enemies. The media, big tech, and Congress are providing aid and comfort to those enemies.

They have become the enemy of the people. Countless innocent American lives have been lost because they have failed to keep us safe. So, I'm demanding Congress give me the power to do what they cannot: to save our democracy. Only I can fix it. They know it, you know it, and the American people have had enough. We will not take it anymore!"

President Wolfe continued to sound the alarm and preemptively characterize any attempt to stand in his way, even the very concept of opposition in this time of national emergency, as treason. He outlined a "with us or against us" path to victory that had no patience for nuance, meddling institutions, or partisan politics. If we didn't commit ourselves fully to his vision, we would never rid ourselves of the enemy within, hiding in plain sight—one that was far more dangerous than any external threat.

With only vague whispers of plans to combat the foreign and domestic threats, Wolfe outlined a simple recipe to save the country—give him absolute power. The irony that Wolfe's War Powers Act would dismantle our democracy to save it was lost on a public eager to reclaim its lost sense of security. Many of us saw the Act for the power play it was, but precious few spoke against it. No one wants to be branded a traitor in wartime, but, more importantly, we were all scared shitless.

Fear trumped rational thought. We were asked only for our faith. It was easy.

While many did not believe Wolfe's contention that he was democracy incarnate, the embodiment of popular will, even the most cerebral were disposed to believe drastic times called for drastic measures. It pains me to admit it now, but I voted for him and supported the Act. I reckoned if we needed a dictator to weather the storm ahead, Wolfe would do. His incendiary speech shocked me, but I assumed it was theatrics to rally the nation. I assured myself that he would relinquish power when the imminent danger had passed.

Wolfe had come to power as a common-sense centrist, the antithesis of the corrupt and polarized major parties. The populace embraced Wolfe's Act to jettison a two-party system it deemed irreversibly ineffective, unaccountable, and inaccessible.

I witnessed the inaccessible part firsthand. Marty, a long-time family friend, failed spectacularly in politics after spending half of his life savings running for school board. I volunteered for his campaign.

"I'm sorry, Jane," he told me days before the election. "I wasted your time, sweetheart. We couldn't afford the spots. Our pamphlets weren't as nice. We didn't have a cool logo." He slowly hissed out "cool logo" between clenched teeth.

The experience made him bitter. He lost faith in democracy. He stopped voting.

Marty was a good candidate. But he was an independent with ideas, not money, at a time when the campaign that spent the most won 97 percent of elections. Marty was outspent, invisible, and deemed "not serious."

We were at a tipping point when novel ideas, good candidates, and thoughtful voters could not escape the gravity well of the two-party system, horserace media, and big-money donors. That black hole of political dysfunction amplified cynicism and polarization to a fever pitch. Nothing could be heard above the din of hyper-hyperbole.

Eventually, the noise became too loud for party moderates like Marty, who either followed the party exodus to the fringes or joined a growing number of centrists in the political wilderness. Year after year, they voted for the least-worst option or stopped voting altogether. They watched the fabric of the nation tear wider and deeper—into a bottomless chasm by the 2028 election.

I was one of them. We quietly became the independent majority, albeit a majority of no consequence. The party duopoly remained safe behind their gamed system. We were ripe for the picking.

Candidate Wolfe was one of a small handful of citizens rich enough to run for president without a party. He was already popular. He owned his own media, social media, and digital network. Wolfe cast himself as a humble public servant compelled to save the country from itself. He vowed to "return to Silicon Valley, doing the work I love" the day after a single term.

If it was a trap, who could blame us for falling into it? The alternative was assured and accelerated national decline. As Wolfe's campaign gained momentum, it pulled in zombie partisans and apathetic non-voters. He won big. We thought we won too.

Then the war came. Desperate to remain relevant, politicians at all levels and from both parties fell all over each other to voice loud, unreserved support for Wolfe's War Powers Act, despite the long-term cost to their own power.

The Act gave Wolfe unbridled powers. He closed the physical and digital borders. No person or idea allowed in or out.

Buried in the War Powers Act, which no one in Congress bothered to read, were Trojan Horse provisions to expand the Supreme Court to thirteen members and allow it to "propose changes to make legislation consistent with its intent." President Wolfe immediately appointed the four new justices, and his inner circle would feed the new Court its cases and rulings.

Within the year, the Court ruled that, although the First Amendment forbade any single law "prohibiting the free exercise of speech," multiple laws were not addressed and therefore allowed. Regarding the Second Amendment's right to arms, it reasoned that "arms" did not include ammunition or preclude the government from installing "safety" devices to monitor citizen weaponry. It ruled that a blanket warrant authorizing government searches was consistent with Fourth Amendment search requirements to specify "place, persons, and things to be seized" because it applied without prejudice or specificity to "all citizens, all homes, everywhere." The rulings were all bullshit, but the veneer of legalistic word salad legitimized them to the weak-minded.

President Wolfe controlled the Supreme Court, and the Court controlled Congress. He consolidated public institutions, media, business, and civil society under the Goliath Network "for efficiency and safety." Leaders from all sectors quickly fell in line, correctly ascertaining that maintaining their positions depended on fealty to Wolfe.

President Wolfe would be the last president to win a legitimate election. Transition day, from Wolfe's speech to the late-night vote passing the Act, lasted less than 48 hours. As it neared two-and-a-half centuries, our ailing democratic experiment died with a sigh of relief from the masses and a whimper from the few of us who protested.

It was all legal because the Supreme Court said it was. It was all reasonable because the Goliath Network said it was. It all made sense because we wanted to believe. We needed a savior.

Any lingering opposition ceased to exist midway through the second year of the war, when Congress was dissolved in favor of the Council of the Americas, which included our new countrymen from South and Central America. The Council passed the new Inter-American Constitution in a month. Council committees divided up judicial and legislative responsibilities and granted the Goliath Network supreme executive power. A few years later, the Network appointed a new Council itself.

The next morning, I protested to any friend, coworker, or passing stranger within earshot that "Goliath stole our vote!" Later that day, Ted, my supervisor, dropped by my office, sat on the edge of my desk, and smiled at me as if to a malcontented child. I steeled myself for a reprimand.

"So, I understand you don't get how the Council works." Ted proceeded to explain with agonizing condescension how the Goliath Network based the assignments on aggregate citizen preferences and, therefore, were "more democratic than voting in person." I had a hard time reconciling Ted's awkward pro-Goliath outreach with his pre-transition day self, when he was a party stalwart adamantly opposed to President Wolfe. Now Ted was all in for Wolfe, Goliath, or anything else that might get him promoted.

I nodded approvingly to his points and enthusiastically added that using Network projections to elect officials would also "force 100 percent voter turnout." Lucky for me, the sarcasm was lost on Ted. My faux change of heart likely convinced him not to recommend a social merit reduction.

"Now you've got it!" He beamed proudly. Having fixed his errant employee, Ted smugly jumped off my desk and was out the door.

That's how Goliath completed its takeover and how I learned to keep my mouth shut.

June 25

I spent much of today thinking about yesterday's entry, trying to identify the turning point that led us to this unimaginable place. It was not transition day. That was merely the public playing out of hidden agendas—political performance art. The forces that set that day in motion were seeded in the minds of men much, much earlier.

It started benignly enough with tools to help us think, organize, remember: the abacus, the calendar, cave drawings. But as civilization advanced and the tools evolved, they slowly began to replace instead of assist. They did the thinking; we became the tools.

When we started to rely on the technology to remember for us, the door was opened. At that point, the Network was free to recreate the world, unchained from facts or accountability. With no sources to contradict it, pasts were rewritten in real time to support whatever present Goliath desired. How would anyone know differently? Truth became the exclusive domain of Goliath, locked behind its firewalls.

I vaguely remember early social media linked you up with people you knew. Even before transition day, it became the main way to get to know people, how they got to know you, how you got a job, how you found a spouse, where you shopped for goods and information. That transformation is almost absolute now. Why waste time on off-liners who can't be tracked or credited on your account?

People made their own profiles once. Sometimes they exaggerated, sometimes they concealed, sometimes they lied. But it belonged to them.

After transition day, one of my thousand "close" social media friends changed her profile image to a harmless anti-war message: "choose peace." I thought she was a naïve peacenik. We had to fight back, at least for a while. But I liked the general sentiment that we should strive for peace.

I tried to copy it as my profile image, but it wouldn't post. I kept trying, hitting the enter key repeatedly and harder, as one does. After three or four tries, I chalked it up as a Network glitch and forgot about it. The next morning, as I ate breakfast under the early morning light of my laptop, I received the same Network announcement we all received: "NETWORK TRAFFIC WILL BE REVIEWED

FOR CONTENT HARMFUL TO THE WAR EFFORT
OR PUBLIC GOOD."

I did not think much of it. It seemed reasonable. What kind
of person posts against the public good? I did not understand
that I was already one of those people, that it had blocked
my attempt to change my profile image. It was harmful. I was
harmful.

I went to my friend's page. Her "choose peace" image was
replaced with "support our troops." My heart skipped a beat,
and I started to sweat. Things had changed, and I was being
cast to the other side of the good and evil digital divide.

I was alarmed but assumed it would be temporary. That was
more than thirty years ago.

June 26

It has been cathartic to write down my transition memories. I feel like the part of my brain tasked with faithfully maintaining those recollections could finally relax. After so many years, it felt good to write with my own hands again.

I'd been afraid to document it on the Network. For starters, it would be autocorrected to comply with Goliath history. The Network could flag me as a miscreant and suspend my authoring privileges for "misinformation." I'd still be fed information, but my ability to send would be silenced. Even for family and friends, I'd cease to exist for a time. Worst case, my rantings would be taken more seriously, and I'd cease to exist forever.

While unburying those long-repressed memories was liberating, it also provoked a singular question that haunted me all day: why? Why did a free people choose to forsake their freedoms? Why do we continue to follow Goliath?

Most of us did not see a downside to the growing dominance of technology and entertainment. We heralded artificial intelligence's role in exponentially merging and growing that dominance. I too embraced the new trinity of AI, technology, and entertainment.

Our trust in the Network was richly rewarded. The advantages were hard to argue with. Goliath put an end to the "he said, she said" world of perceptions. Everything was known. Every event was captured.

It was comforting. It was easy. We were relieved to be told what to do, what to think, where to go. Since its commands were ostensibly "suggestions" based on our Network history, we convinced ourselves it was, ultimately, still us pulling the strings.

Personal memory, critical analysis, and independent opinion atrophied, burdens of a bygone era. Only Goliath, an entity of pure data unhindered by human failings, could be trusted.

Goliath became the one true God for a people wary of old beliefs. Divine truth would no longer be the purview of human charlatans to transcribe and misinterpret from the mouth of God. It would come directly from the source.

But it lied about David's death; it lied about me. That ignited a fire to expose its deceits. People need to know the truth.

I am not so foolish as to document the lies of this false god on its own instrument, the Network, which means I rely on what pen and paper I still have. Handwriting is allowed with stylus on screen, like any kind of art, but its off-Network use is untraceable and, thus, technically illegal. Simply keeping this journal makes me something of a bush league criminal.

Maybe I'll never have the evidence I need to release this journal, but it serves another purpose. It may be the only genuine part of me I leave behind. I want to be understood by anyone who reads it.

Assuming the Network does' just delete me, please do not believe the Goliath version of me. The Network version of anyone is not really them.

June 27

Lily stopped by today, shortly before I had to leave for work. She lives a few blocks away in Peaceful Yearning, the name of my neighborhood of low-merit castaways.

I opened the door and provided the standard "Goliath morning" greeting. The smiling teenager reached into her pack. "I wanted to give these back before school."

I grabbed her arm and asked her to step inside.

"Lily, you must remember not to show books in public," I admonished. "People will think you are weird."

"Oh, I don't care, Ms. Jane." She shrugged. Lily and her small group of friends genuinely didn't care. Living at the bottom of the social ladder gave the youth in Peaceful Yearning little to lose or form jealousies about. They bonded over their common poverty. The privileges Goliath used to control us reinforced their rebelliousness. That would change in time, but I enjoyed seeing it.

Lily handed me the three books I lent her and ran off.

"Thanks for the books, Ms. Jane," she blurted out over her shoulder on my doorstep.

"Not so loud, podster!" I cried. I understood she didn't care about demerits from nosy neighbors, but I could not lose from plain carelessness.

We are called podsters because we live in modular pod houses on small plots. It's a pejorative term others call us, and we sometimes call ourselves. Modern-day trailer trash.

The basic pod structure is three circular-domed units connected by short walkways, one each for a kitchen, living room, and combination bathroom/laundry/storage pod. Goliath adds pods if your social merit score goes up.

Lily and her mom, Becky, have the additional bedroom pod but almost no windows. I prefer to spend my merit on windows, but I live alone. I am always on the edge of getting or losing a separate bedroom pod but don't really care. I'm fine sleeping in the living room. Once, I had bedroom and garage pods, but my score hasn't been that high for years.

Lily finally returned Walden after months. It was a favorite among my group of oldbook eccentrics. "Oldbook" has become the replacement word for book, since there are no such things as new books. The younger tech-weary members were drawn to Walden's embrace of nature as an alternative to Goliath life. Its popularity was showing in the wear to the book's cover and spine. I had to remind the frequent borrowers to treat it more carefully.

A high school history book about the old United States, a far less popular loaner, came to me in the same batch of books. Once I realized its value, I stopped sharing it. How I came across those books revealed the dangerous race I am in to find off-Network evidence before Goliath destroys it. The experience made me double down on collecting old books, news reports, and government records that contradicted Goliath Network narratives. I will explain more tomorrow.

June 28

As I began investigating my brother's death, I thought I might find some clues at the archives. I used to love going to the Document Archive Regional Center in Seattle, the only public place where physical books still existed. Books were always my escape. I clung to them ever more addictively the rarer they became.

I remember how the smell of books would rush over me as I walked into libraries as a kid. Like a coffee addict smelling the morning roast, it would trigger cascades of dormant synapses in my brain. I anticipated the limitless experiences, perspectives, and worlds authors provided through their books. Directly from them. Directly to me. I wanted to read them all.

Even as a kid, though, I sensed the end of books was coming. My friends preferred their screens and found books increasingly tiresome. People gradually stopped saying, "The movie is OK, but you should really read the book." It's a nonsensical saying now, with the near extinction of books.

Not long after the war started, artificial intelligence developed the ability to turn books into movies and did so en masse. A few years later, it was able to create three-dimensional holographic versions of the books. If hooked up to cerebral implants, these virtual reality experiences could invade all our senses: simulating smells, tastes, and even touch.

The CGI-5D immersive format, or 5D as it was commonly called, soon subsumed all entertainment and information programming. The battle David died in was briefly mentioned in the news before the anchor segued by saying, "You can learn more about it on 5D." I spent a week's wages to watch an account of the battle called Blue-Green 5-2038: Operation Valorous Shield. Lots of drama among the soldiers, edge-of-seat action, and blowing up of things, but nothing useful about the battle itself.

I took notes on the use of unit, place, and soldier names to research at the archive. It was a long shot, since I had no idea whether anything in the movie was actually "based on a true story," but I'd hoped to pull some facts from the nebulous ether of that horrible movie. It was also an excuse to visit the closest thing left to a library.

A few of us mourned the consolidations and closures of libraries, but most viewed the end of oldbooks as progress. "Bookworm" became a strongly derogatory term reserved for losers like me with an odd fixation for dated technology. Like the photography fanatics who stockpiled film before they stopped making it, I hoarded books as they became increasingly scarce, trading them with others similarly afflicted.

I had not been to the archive for years. It was nearly 80 miles away, a costly journey given my chronically low social merit score. After I set my one-seater hover down in an almost empty lot, I paused in anticipation before making my way through the big, old-fashioned glass doors of the archive. I enjoyed the simple pleasure of pulling the door manually, hearing the hinge creek—a rare exception to the automated swish of modern doors. I expected the familiar smell of old books to greet me like an old friend.

I was crushed to find the archive in complete disarray. Where rows of bookshelves spread to the distant walls of the cavernous warehouse, now there were only a couple columns of shelves huddled to the right of the entrance. Only a small fraction of the archive stock remained, surrounded like wolves by shipping crates. The long c-shaped help desk was still pinned against the wall near the door but was entirely abandoned, save a lone packer propped up on it, eating his lunch.

I bolted to the remaining shelves, where workers were sealing up a crate of books. I saw someone through three columns of empty shelves inventorying a shelf that was still full. He was busily moving books into boxes as I repeatedly tapped his shoulder like a woodpecker.

"Hello," he said calmly as he turned. "Who are you? I'm not expecting a shipment."

I told him I wasn't there about a shipment. I was there for the archives. I demanded to know what happened to the archives.

"Oh, you found them," he said, pausing for a moment with a wry, welcoming grin as he pushed his floating inventory screen to the side. "Are you actually looking for something from the archive?"

"Yes, yes I am," I replied curtly, swaying between disbelief and outrage. I tried to calmly explain that I came to do research, mostly failing with the calm part. I asked where the hell all the books were being moved to.

"Moved to?" he asked back. "Look, what you see is what's left, and that's moving alright, moving to the incinerator." He laughed under his breath at the quip but quickly changed character when he saw me wince. Besides losing a chance to figure out what happened to David, my favorite place on planet Earth was being dissected before my eyes.

His nonchalant façade evaporated. He tried to reassure me that he was "not happy about it either." To cheer me up, he lightheartedly introduced himself as "Brian, the archive's last librarian, or Li-Brian for short."

Brian explained that after the Network finished scanning the books, government records, and something called microfiche from all the archives, it decided preserving physical copies was redundant. Archive staff were reassigned to oversee the logging of archives for destruction and slowly reassigned to other vocations.

Brian was, in fact, the last librarian standing at the Seattle archive. A young man without a family, he said he could afford the cut in merit points with the demotion and wanted "to make sure it was done right." Sensing his statement could be mistaken for enthusiasm to burn books, he clarified what he meant was a duty to see the old books and papers "respectfully retired."

I had misjudged him.

Brian wanted to talk more, but there was nothing else to say. I meekly thanked him and walked out. I held it together until turning down the alley between the old archive building and a neighboring weather station. I wasn't ready to drive, so I leaned my back against the building.

Movers pushed crates of books by me, suspended on hoverboards like a funeral procession. Authors made immortal

by their works could cheat death no more. I felt silly for
crying about what most would dismiss as taking out the
trash. Worse, I lost a chance to find leads in David's case.
I looked at the ground, hoping it would swallow me whole.

It occurred to me that books were not merely trending
out with the times—this was deliberate. The Network
could have just had the books thrown out; there was no need
to meticulously catalogue their destruction. A printed page
represented an independent source of information beyond
Goliath's digital control. Books were a threat to its power.

"I'm glad I found you here," a warm voice above me said.
It was Brian. I sat up and wiped my watering eyes.

"I can talk freely here," he explained. "This passageway
between the buildings is a signal dead zone and
camera-free." He took a knee and dropped the small box he
was carrying with a thud between us. It was full of books.
He asked me to keep it. I shook my head half-heartedly to
reject the offer, fearing a trap.

"You're not crazy, Jane," he said, touching my shoulder.
Unapproved touching was a risky and punishable act,
making the near stranger's outreach all the more
remarkable. He wrote something in one of the books, left
the box, and walked away.

I realize now he was smuggling archives out, one small
box at a time. A fellow subversive.

I wasn't ready for that conversation. It took me days to process. But even as Brian walked away, I felt a sense of possibility and purpose I had not felt since before the war—hope.

The chance encounter assured me I wasn't insane. I was right to keep pushing. There were others.

June 29

Today was a shit show. I organized a small group of neighbors in our low-income neighborhood to protest the building of a weather station across the street. They parked a huge construction imager there over the weekend to start work Monday.

The imager was about the size of a 20-story building and towered over the tiny shipping container-like modules we lived in. The imager would hover over the site and slowly print the half-mile wide cement base that the two-mile high shining metal obelisk would sit on. Once completed, we'd be listening to the intrusive roar of ion cannons charging and firing into the atmosphere at all odd hours.

Replication technology had long ago replaced many craftsmen and taken over small-scale manufacturing. Construction workers once thought they were essential. They might still think that as they loiter around work sites, ostensibly "supervising" Network AI as it directs the replication of ever larger structures.

They dutifully inspect and check off every step in the process, from site selection to drafting plans to imaging each brick, cable, and pipe together. But as their skills and experience atrophied, our engineers were in no position to second-guess the Goliath Network's collective intelligence—beyond human comprehensive and without human error. It would be like correcting God. They were like kids playing with a giant 3D printer, except the imager pressed its own buttons.

I would normally feel pity for them. They think a title and willingness to work somehow give their work meaning, where there is none. But today, they are the enemy, and I feel nothing but contempt for the arrogant, ignorant sons of bitches.

A dozen of us blocked access to the elevator at the machine's base that brings the crew to the control booth on top. The crew didn't much care. They were getting paid regardless. After about an hour, a two-seater hovercraft thrusted wildly into the equipment yard and came to an angry, sliding stop about ten feet from our group.

The driver sprang out and made a beeline directly to me, somehow knowing I was the organizer. The sharply-suited man with slicked-back hair started pointing at me accusingly before his words caught up. He was trying to be measured and calm, but he was having a hard time not taking a swing at me then and there.

"Look, you and your people need to clear out of here now! Got it? You have no right to be here. You are interfering with Goliath infrastructure improvements." I suppose he thought that would be the end of it because he put his six-shooter finger back into its pocket holster, stepped back, and smugly leaned back against the hover, waiting for us to leave.

"No, this is bullshit," I retorted loudly. I matched his fury and physical tension. I talk with my hands too, only I was chopping the air with both hands to my sides.

"You're the one who has no right to be here, fucking bureaucrat. This land was zoned as a forest, and the law says you can't build here. So, move this shit out, and let us have our forest back! Got it?"

He wasn't expecting that. None of them knew what to say. All that yelling and then dead silence for about ten seconds.

He looked away from me at the imager to gather his thoughts. A moment later, he turned back and pulled a projection drone from his forearm iCom. He set it to float, pushed the square-inch floating drone between us, and activated a five-foot by three-foot projection of an official-looking document to the side so we could all see it.

"I'm going to blow this up some, so you all understand," he patronized. He looked at us but through us, as if we were not worthy of direct eye contact. He had regained his composure some but was still smoldering with contempt for my band of misfits that had made him trek out beyond the edge of town. We probably ruined his golf game or cut short his morning triple shot macchiato.

He turned and pointed to the document's title: "PARCEL 451: Legal Use."

"As you can clearly see, this is the zoning ordinance for this land, issued way back in 2038." He paused, scrolled down, and zoomed in on a passage near the middle of the document as if he were pulling up a snake from the ground to kill it. "Read this part, where it says what? Zoned for forest? No sir! What does it say?"

"Zoned for weather station," said Bill meekly from the back, not quite sure whether the question was rhetorical or not. "Big Bill" was an imposing 6'5" giant who was standing tall against injustice seconds ago. Bill's indignation deflated to fear in the face of "facts" brought by the foreman, or project supervisor, or public affairs specialist... He never told us his name or position.

"That's right, my good man!" The bureaucrat smiled like a laser in Bill's direction, a form of reward to make the others crack. "Now that you realize you were wrong, please go home and we'll forget this ever happened."

There was a pregnant pause as he deactivated the projector drone and reattached it to his iCom. He looked back over at us, realizing the group was quietly waiting for him to complete the thought, too scared to ask the question directly.

"Oh yes, if you leave now, no social merit will be deducted. It's clear you were just misinformed. No harm done. Off you go!"

Half the crowd left, relieved to escape unpenalized. The document was obviously faked. I wasn't ready to walk away. Five others stayed with me, unsure if they should surrender as well.

"Hold on. This isn't right. I found the ordinance. It was always for protected forest. What are we going to do with a loud-ass weather station here? These people don't live next to a fancy park and can't go on fancy vacations. You can't take our forest away from us!"

I don't remember exactly what I said, but that was close. I had tried to be convincing, but it sounded desperate and confused because *I was* desperate and confused. Still, it was enough for the five to stand pat and for Bill to stop walking away and turn back for a moment. Bill spent most of his free time in the forest. It was his sanctuary, his church.

"Oh, my dear, Ms. Veristo," he patronized, assured that I posed no further threat. "Do calm down. You know we need the weather stations. We don't want to return to the burning times. Do *you*?"

With that, Bill continued back home. I pulled up my iCom to frantically find the ordinance, my proof he was lying. I found it. Or, rather, I found the document he had shown us in the place where the original zoning document had been bookmarked.

The Network official guessed what I was frantically searching for but waited until my face dropped in disbelief before administering the coup de grâce.

"I told you." He shook his head while crossing his arms with practiced condescension. He smugly leaned back, done talking. The trap was sprung. He was waiting for me to concede.

"It's OK, Jane," said Becky. "We were wrong. You saw it yourself. It was zoned that way all along." The others walked away.

I hesitated a few moments, weighing my options briefly to delay my defeat. Finally, I ran to join my neighbors down the path that led from the construction yard to the main road.

"Stupid cunt," the man with the slick hair sneered quietly enough that only I could hear it.

I could have mentioned I had shots of the original documents saved on an old stand-alone camera. I could have escalated the matter, but I wanted to pick my battles. He knew my name. Mentioning it was a warning.

I added the original zoning papers to my vast evidence stash. I told myself that eventually my proof of all the small lies would snowball into a mass so heavy that even the most compliant of citizens could not resist its gravity. Once they finally recognized the truth, they would push the truth back into Goliath and smash it to bits.

I ate a light lunch. This morning's defeat at the hands of the nameless bureaucrat had robbed me of an appetite. As I nibbled, I monitored my social merit score in the upper right-hand corner of my house screens. He said there would be no demerits, but I feared it just the same.

As I rose to clean the kitchen, I saw a flicker out of the corner of my eye. My score dropped 135 points. I dropped my plate on the floor.

For this futile attempt to tilt at the windmills, I had already wasted a leave day. The penalty cut the rest of my meager leave allotment in half. I lost access to some nicer foods and premium channels. No watching with friends—the iCom blocks transmissions within thirty feet.

But the transportation downgrade is the one that really hurts. I am now under threshold for a hovercraft. I will have to turn in my small craft for a hoverbike. I will strap groceries to the steering bar and maybe attach a rear basket. I will have to wear a heavy coat to work. I won't be able to take anyone anywhere. My ability to leverage likes from others will suffer with the lower score, compounding the damage. As they say, "You have to have merit credit to make merit credit." At least I aged out of military conscription, the ultimate punishment for going into the merit score red.

I suspect I will be the only one punished. Goliath knows my neighbors will see my tiny bike and at least wonder if I deserved it. Not punishing the whole group rewards their complicity and makes me the other.

I cried in utter frustration, off and on, throughout the afternoon. My iCom chimed, snapping me out of despair. It was Lily, Becky's 14-year-old daughter, staring up at me with a sympathetic smile. We sat at the two chairs at my small kitchen table. Lily got right to the point.

"My mom told me all about the stand-off at the site today. I guess we're going to get a storm factory out here after all. Just fantastic," she rattled off, pausing at the end to let the sarcasm sink in.

"Look, Ms. Jane, I saw the original zoning papers too, same as you, same as my mom. They are lying and think we are too brainwashed, or scared, or lazy, or whatever to say anything. Well, I'm calling bullshit. My mom might be OK with it, but I'm the hell not!"

Sweet, timid Lily had worked herself up. We talked for more than an hour. Those words were like oxygen to my asphyxiated soul. Sometimes, younger people give me hope and make me think the truth is still worth fighting for. Older people are trained to deny inconvenient truths. The youth naturally seek the truth and don't yet understand why it should be repressed.

The young are also generally disposed to rebel against parents and their conformist ways. There's something compelling to youth about old rebels who have not fully tempered their passions. For the first time in years, I felt vindicated, maybe even a little cool.

June 30

Reading through my previous entries, I realize I've made it sound like no one did anything to stand in Goliath's path. The Network erased all memory of those who stood up to it. I've done no better to honor them but will try to fix that today. Yes, most people went along with Wolfe's transition day, but it was far from unanimous.

Many early Wolfe critics were drafted after the war started. Others disappeared. Many simply gave up. I turned the guilt of ignoring warning signs into a frantic resistance as Goliath rolled out. I joined a movement.

Eight months into the Goliath experiment, there was still some residual resistance to it. People remained in the habit of expressing dissenting opinions without consequence. New habits would prevail, but it was still early.

By that time, we finally realized that online protests were easily ignored, co-opted, or deleted, and invariably used to identify "enemy agents." Virtual protests were merely bytes for the government to distort or feed into the digital abyss.

We decided to organize an old-timey protest with flesh-and-blood people. It would target the Supreme Court in DC, amplified regionally at federal courthouses across the nation. Signs and banners would protest the war, of course, but also the home-front erosion of rights.

My friend Gloria was a key local organizer. She was also an IT mastermind. She effortlessly surfed the codes behind the screens that were just black magic to me.

She showed up the day before the protest, repeatedly striking the doorbell. I flung the door open wide to reveal a short waif of a girl who was thirty but could pass for thirteen. Her hands nervously clenched and unclenched her crossed arms as she swayed from side to side. Despite her café con leche Latina complexion, Gloria was white as a sheet. Her eyes stared blankly through my chest.

"What's wrong?" I asked. I expected some benign organizational issue with the protest had her worked up.

"I couldn't call," she said, answering a question I had not asked. "I want you to have this." She reached in her sweatshirt pocket but stopped herself before pushing me back through my doorway and closing the door behind us.

"Take it." She pulled a tattered, white envelope from her pocket and thrust it into my dangling hand, releasing it the millisecond I grabbed it, as if it were toxic.

"What is it? What happened?" I pleaded.

Gloria was normally cool and unflappable. Her panicked state unnerved me and infected me. I held the small envelope gingerly between my thumb and pointer finger. It felt somehow heavier than it was.

"I fucked up, Jane," she said without emotion, still looking through me. "I tried to override the protocols to post about the protest. I wanted to spread the word. I thought it was important. It worked—for a few minutes. Then, the posts went down. Then my computer went down."

She paused for a moment to look out the small window in my front door.

"I started getting calls. I let it ring. I threw a few things in my pack and ran."

She abruptly cut herself off and looked at her archaic mechanical watch, snapping her head down and up again in a nervous instant. She wasn't wearing her iCom. "It doesn't matter. I don't matter. This ..."

She struggled for words, nervously fidgeting her fingers against each other. She was always more fluent in computer languages than human communication, but never like this.

Finally, she looked into my eyes for the first time and found her voice.

"Maybe it will help." She motioned her head toward the envelope. "It's all my hacked data on the new Network. Mostly technical stuff—how it absorbed competing networks. But also how it influences people, tells them what to do. Bad things, Jane. How it lied. How it punished people who would not play along."

A barely visible smirk cracked through her paralyzed face. A hint of color returned to her cheeks. She slowed down for a moment of satisfied pride. "I did it, Jane. I figured it out."

The fear and 500-mile stare suddenly returned. "Good luck. Be careful with it. Goodbye, Jane," she said in a choppy, machine-gun pace before spinning around, flinging the door open, and bolting away.

I stood there for minutes afterward, staring through the open door, trying to make sense of the bizarre encounter. I wondered if Gloria would return that night or if I'd ever see her again. I thought of all the things I could have said, assurances I could have made to keep my troubled friend from melting down. I didn't give her the embrace she so desperately needed.

My friend deserved more than my shock and confusion. But it was academic—too late. She was gone. I tried to call her, but her profile was offline. Later, it would disappear entirely. They deleted her.

I was afraid for Gloria and my other dissident friends. I wasn't a leader, but I was still afraid for myself. What had she gotten me into?

I smothered those personal concerns to focus on the protest, the same protest Gloria was trying to publicize for the following morning. It might be our last chance to put the world back in order while it could still be saved. I owed it to Gloria to at least show up.

Spread by word of mouth, I was surprised at the large crowd. At least four thousand brave souls gathered at the Seattle Courthouse. I was late enough that I was only at the edge of the group when hundreds of police charged in, arresting those on the periphery as they peeled away layers to get to the protest's nucleus.

Electrons like me, still circling ambiguously beyond the demonstration's edge, had a choice to make. Move toward the protest's core and get arrested or pretend to be bystanders and go home. I chose the latter. I survived. I never heard from my friends in that protest again.

That night, it was on the news. At a press conference, President Wolfe said it was "a reminder of how enemy misinformation can mobilize radicals against their own government." Not one critical question. No one spoke up for us.

I noticed the White House press corps was different. All the reporters who used to ask pointed questions about the war were gone. I remembered how a reporter had asked a few days into the war whether a communications blackout between deployed troops and their family members was really necessary.

"Why do you want to put crosshairs on our troops, Bret?" the president fired back. "Private Ruby Fish called home, and the enemy got the drop on her unit's position. Now Ruby's dead. People like you killed her. You need to say her name. Say her name!"

This president would not abide by the position's past practice or decorum. He used press conferences to bully and attack, not to explain. Some decried his style as beneath the office. But most celebrated it as "keeping it real."

"Say her name" became the evening headline. The story became the reporter's threat to operations security, or OPSEC. The next day, some old messages were unearthed of the reporter expressing sexist, unpatriotic views. Pundits called for his resignation. They got it.

Only the next day did I remember the envelope. I hid it in the rafters of my unfinished basement and forgot about it. I would understand its significance in the days and weeks to come.

It remains in my evidence cache, along with a stand-alone system that can read it. I don't understand all the technical stuff, but the evil embedded between the codes and commands is clear to anyone who can read English.

July 1

Caleb Rater holo-messaged me today. He only reaches out on-Network to set up in-person, off-Network conversations. A projection of his big head hovered over my iCom.

"Jane, I'll meet you at the same spot along the river as last year. Let's try to get there close to sunup. 6:45, Sunday after next. See you there."

He assumed I could make it. He didn't even look up while recording. He takes me entirely for granted.

Caleb is from my old circle of college friends, mostly journalism majors. He's the only one I keep in any kind of regular contact with. Most of them moved up the social merit food chain and disassociated from me—unfriended, in the old social media parlance.

A few will call me out of the blue, mostly to talk vacuously about old times. Then I don't hear from them for months, even years. My low Social Merit Indicator scores would bring down their SMIs and send their algorithm careening off course.

Every spring, Caleb reaches out to arrange a bird watching outing or two, as is our decades-long ritual. Caleb enjoys our outings enough to risk the small hit to his incredibly high score. But I hardly hear from him the rest of the year, minimizing his exposure.

I'm not sure if I'm a pity friend or if he's just so fanatical about his hobby that I'm a necessary evil. I minored in ornithology. I teach him bird stuff.

Goliath tells us it has "liberated" us from work, want, and religion. With the advent of free fusion energy, sustainable food and water, industrial automation, and medical breakthroughs, many of the hardships that required a workforce evaporated. People don't need to rely on family anymore. They don't complain about politics or health.

Pastimes and hobbies have become what people talk about, how they identify themselves. When you ask Caleb what he does, he'll tell you he is president of a prominent birding organization.

Caleb is a bellwether for me. If I'm ever to convince people to doubt the Network, I'll need to start with people like Caleb, who had been a Wolfe skeptic before the transition. I test the waters every year. Early on, when iComs were still removable, we'd walk for hours and talk more frankly about things, about the past, even about Goliath.

I tried to bring up our mutual friends, Laura Redden and Desmond Aparicido, a couple years after they disappeared. The three of them started out at the same local television news station. Laura and Des married and, after a few years, moved on to prominent media jobs in New York.

The conversation did not go well.

"Do you ever hear from Laura?" I asked.

Caleb pretended not to hear, looking intently for a cardinal through thick branches. I asked again.

"No, I don't," he said flatly, still looking.

"Does she still write?" I asked. Lauren stuck with print journalism, despite the poor pay and small audience. He turned to face me.

"Last I heard, she was doing technical writing on appliance manuals. I have not talked to her since Des deployed."

Des was at the peak of his popularity when he went off to war, hosting a national news program. Des had taken the leap from journalism to punditry. His fans were called Des's Denizens. He was influential. His opinion mattered.

Des had taken a hard stand against the War Powers Act for weeks after transition day. He challenged all the made-up facts and dubious war narratives. Then, suddenly, he said he'd been wrong. In a highly-viewed final show, he said he regretted "providing comfort to the enemy."

"I can never undo what I've done," he said in a tone oddly both anxious and monotone. "But I will make it right. I'm enlisting."

I tried to reach out to my celebrity friend and his wife but had no luck. A few weeks later, a special was aired of Des with his new unit on the front, fighting back a combined Green and Red forces offensive. Des said little beyond agreeing with the Goliath News Network interviewers. He was a zombie prop in GNN's narrative about a reformed patriot.

GNN had absorbed all media as the "one voice" for the emerging new United States. It eventually took over media from other South and Central American states, as those governments were convinced to join us. Incentivized by access to our vaccines for the new Ebola strains, they all eventually joined the United Hemispheres of America in the Global War on Evil (GWoE).

Although the term forever war was initially banned, along with transition day, Goliath eventually allowed and even socialized the concept. It became sloganized and cycled through our feeds:

EVIL IS WITH US FOREVER. WE MUST FIGHT IT FOREVER. FOREVER WAR PROTECTS US FOREVER!

"What do you think happened to Des?" I asked Caleb. That special report was the last we'd seen of him.

"I don't know, Jane." He stopped recording a nest of finches, turned off his iCom, and paused as if contemplating something meaningful but diverted back to "I just don't know. He served his country." Caleb turned down the riverside path, trying to end the conversation.

"I don't think so," I snapped back, hoping to snap him back with me. "I think they forced him into it. Maybe threatened his family. The whole thing smells like horseshit."

"Maybe," said Caleb, over his shoulder. "Maybe not. We'll never know. At least we'll remember him as a hero."

"More like a zero."

"Are you trying to be a bitch? Jesus! A little respect, please."

"That's not what I meant," I explained. "There's nothing on him in the records anymore after transition day. Zero. It's like it never happened."

Caleb seemed surprised. "That's not possible."

"There is only a record of his show ending the day before the transition. Nothing about those post-transition shows. I have hard copies—"

"Be careful!" he cut me off.

When I mentioned using the tapes against the Network, he became flustered, almost angry.

"OK, no. You need to stop!" Now, I was the surprised one. "What do you think you've got there? Video doesn't prove shit. 2D? Ha! They will just say you manipulated the video. AI could do that in a hot minute."

He was not wrong.

I wanted to tell him about the wet film I had of old documents the Network lied about or denied even existed, about negatives I had of the old Constitution. Those couldn't be forged. Darkroom photography turned out to be a useful hobby after all.

"Forget about it, Jane. Look ..." He shook his head before locking eyes with me. "I'm going to tell you the truth about Laura. She wasn't a crusader like her husband. All she wanted to do was write. She wasn't smart enough to have opinions. They let her continue with her job after Des deployed. I'm not even sure she knew it wasn't his idea."

My eyes widened. I took in all this inside baseball from a guy who just insisted he didn't know anything about it.

"But it didn't help her, did it?" he asked rhetorically. "They told her to stop publishing crime statistics. Simple! But she did it anyway. That's why they fired her ass!"

Dumbfounded, I tried to connect the dots Caleb was laying out for me. My uncharacteristic silence frustrated him.

"Don't you understand why I'm telling you this, dumbass?" He raised his head to the sky with a full-body eye roll.

"Look, don't be a Laura, OK? Stop this straight-arrow crap. It doesn't matter what you have, Jane. No one is going to believe you. They will believe Goliath. It saved them from every threat—the war, the warming, the pandemics. Goliath is their god! You need to accept that."

I have replayed that conversation a thousand times in my head, but I still don't remember exactly what I said back. Caleb said he was done talking about Des and Laura and abruptly started talking about birds again.

Caleb was never again this revealing. He occasionally threw me a sympathetic line when I ranted about Goliath, but always with an "I'm sure there's a good reason for it" disclaimer. "Be careful with that, Jane," he'd say anytime anything remotely close to open subversion came up.

I was never sure how much I could trust Caleb. My suspicion grew as Caleb's fortunes rose. While Des and Laura were banned from journalism, he was elevated to national television, filling a similar role to the one Des vacated. Ambitious or opportunist, maybe it's all the same.

A couple of years back, during one of our hikes, bees were all over the trail. "Good thing Goliath brought back the bees," I commented, mostly to myself. Even I recognized some of the good things Goliath had done. I didn't expect a response.

"Were the bees ever completely gone?" Caleb questioned almost a full minute later as the trail flattened out. "I mean officially?"

"Well, yes," I retorted, not yet understanding what he was getting at. "Rolling out genetically engineered insects to replace extinctions is something Goliath likes to brag about."

"Years ago, maybe," he said. "I'll have to check that. We don't believe that anymore. Genetic modification has fallen out of favor."

I was struck by the notion that he'd have to check the Network record to determine whether something so benign happened or not. My face contorted in dismay at Caleb's nonchalant admission that facts were continually reassessed to determine whether "we" believed in them. Clearly, "we" were not really in charge of what "we" thought anymore.

"History changes so fast these days," I observed, wondering if Caleb could recognize sarcasm anymore.

Caleb seemed part of the machine now. He quickly adhered to the standard Network greeting: "May the Network be with you." I was supposed to reply, "And also with you," but I never did.

Caleb remained a friend, albeit at arm's distance. I imagined he was playing along, but not a true believer. He told me the truth about Laura and Des. He didn't need to do that. Maybe redemption was still possible. Maybe the truth still mattered to him.

July 2

I had to work a double shift today. I don't know why, but I suspect some confidant or neighbor turned me in for anti-social sentiment.

I try to keep my thoughts inside, suppressing my outspoken nature. But things slip now and then. Usually, nothing comes of it.

I try not to think too much about what I said or who might have taken offense. It can drive you crazy and changes nothing. You can only try to be more careful in a world where everyone is on a hair trigger to tank your social merit points and virtue signal their points up. It became the chess game of the new era—all day, every day.

Still, it's hard to know how to improve your game if you can't pinpoint the penalty. Was it a few days back when I told someone leaning on a doorway to pull his head out of his iCom and get the hell out of the way? Interrupting technology is tech-phobic and against the law. Incoming Network communication can convey important government or emergency information, so the iCom always has priority over human interactions.

Even routine Network human-to-human communication is valued over live interactions, which are considered primitive, more difficult, and require imprecise human memory to recall. Talking is still necessary, but the spoken word is an art most do not regard worth honing.

Who complained about me? The most obvious suspect is my sister. I still confide in her without too much filter. I can't fathom her turning me in. We were competitive as kids but always supportive, always honest. Besides, considering what I've told her, the punishment would be far worse than a double shift if she ever turned me in.

If Mary had an issue with me, she would tell me to my face. Most people feel duty-bound to go straight to the Network court of public opinion to flag offensive comments, behavior, or misinformation. And, just like that, your social merit score takes a hit, and you are working a double shift.

Fewer and fewer of my shrinking pool of friends engage at all. Colin and Jay from work like my "before time" stories enough to throw me an occasional invite. But they have to create a groundskeeping-related cover for our outings, so they can log it as "work related." This insulates them from SMI demerits. Since associating with me is a headache, the invites are few and far between.

My sister tells me at least once a month that I'm turning my back on happiness out of stubborn spite to Network progress. Mary thinks my wounds are self-inflected, avoidable battles that will bleed my soul dry. She tries to help me.

Last week, she invited me to "come on over" and "vote with the family."

"An election, what are you talking about?" I replied, not remembering the last political election we had. They were all for show after transition day, weighed to Network polling, which was based on Network exposure. Goliath soon relieved us of the tiresome vestiges of democracy entirely.

"No, silly," Mary explained. "There's at least a couple voting shows tonight, one about singing and another to judge a fight. It'll be fun. Maybe a fashion contest as well. If you don't vote, you can't complain!" Voting in the age of Goliath. Meaningless choices to provide a false sense of agency.

She doesn't get me, but, unlike most everyone else, Mary doesn't give up on people she doesn't understand. I want to believe her constant outreach is genuine love. Or does she only want to keep me from upsetting Mom?

It's risky business to trust someone in the United Hemispheres of America, but I have to trust someone. I want to trust her.

During my double shift, I had lots of time to rehash old grievances. I seethed as I weeded the eco spaces outside the office complex where I used to have a lucrative furniture design job. People mostly stayed in the same area for work. Since it was all Goliath operated, it didn't make sense to move people around.

No one could imagine it now, but there was a lively debate after transition day about free market consolidation. Business owners were told to adopt the "red advantage," which meant consolidating the private sector under Goliath to counter enemy state-supported commercial juggernauts. Adam Marks, founder of grocery giant LifeFood, wanted to keep his regional company independent. He became a public critic of consolidation and the conversion from the dollar to a social merit economy.

Years earlier, when I was a student, I interviewed his son Carl for the university paper after LifeFood financed the football stadium's expansion. I asked him why the grocery giant did not instead invest in the college's agriculture or business schools. He was rattled. After a long pause, he provided some standard speaking points, ignoring the question entirely.

After the interview, he asked for my number. He called me that night, explaining how he wasn't expecting hard questions and rather enjoyed our conversation. He confessed that the donation was pure marketing. People would hear "LifeFood Arena" and see the LifeFood logo at every game. His blunt assessment: "People care about football. No one gives a shit about education. Let the students pay for that."

He lived almost an hour away, and we argued the whole two months we dated. After it ended, Carl would still call me periodically. He missed our arguments and liked my honesty. He called me "no bullshit Jane." He enjoyed a break from his nominal friends, who tended to agree with him without pushback—the rich kid curse most rich kids are too stupid to recognize.

About a month before the transition, he called late in the evening, as was his custom, to complain about his father. Most companies had consolidated by then and were reaping heavy tax rewards for it.

"This fucking dinosaur is killing the company!" he ranted. "We can't compete with the consolidated firms."

I asked him to be a little kinder to his dad, who was, after all, the only reason he was a successful executive.

"Oh, you sassy bitch. That hurts!" he retorted after a roaring laugh.

"OK, it's late, and you are not paying me. I'm hanging up now. Some of us have to work in the morning."

I expected to hear from him within the week, as usual. I never heard from him again.

Months later, following a flurry of scandalous employee complaints, his father stepped down and enlisted for the war effort to redeem himself. The company was consolidated with Goliath. Carl got a promotion.

I miss those honest, playful exchanges, and not only with Carl. Disagreement has become a disagreeable concept, lumped in with terms like hurtful, harmful, and disrespectful—all terms that, if weaponized in a Network complaint, will cost you social merit points. I have learned to steer clear of the misunderstanding minefields of humor, debate, and honest feedback.

It got too dark for weeding, so I went into the gardening shed to organize next year's seeds. Automated systems and sorters had already done the work. I was to "double check" that the seed bins were filled with the right varieties. Upon completion, I would drop an archaic hardcopy checklist on my supervisor's desk.

The computerized seed distributions were never off, of course. Only humans make mistakes. Sometimes, a supervisor would mess with a bin simply to make sure I was doing the work. An easy but mind-numbingly pointless task meant to belittle and punish bad behavior.

Due to my relative hardships, I sometimes forget how easy I have it. Our baseline is far superior to life before transition. Like all citizens, I always have a full stomach, a warm house, and some minimal free time. Our benevolent Goliath Network mostly spares the stick for the carrot—better food, better homes, better opportunities—providing the illusion of fairness and incentives to stay in line. We are slaves to our merit envy.

I stewed in quiet rage as my shift winded down, plotting how I'd triumphantly reestablish my credibility by revealing Goliath's manipulations. The people would see I'd been right all along. The endless indignities would have been worth it. And they would stop.

As I walked to the hoverbay after work, my mind wandered far enough from smug revenge fantasies to let an unsettling truth leak in: Goliath controlled all communication. My master plan to awaken the masses could not use mass communication to do so.

Panic descended. Even an airtight case against Goliath would be meaningless if it couldn't be heard beyond the metal walls of my small pod home. Would I be relegated to spreading my gospel of truth door to door? How long before someone on the other side of one of those doors turned me in? Would Goliath eavesdrop on every seditious word through its iComs?

I became hyper-sensitive to the routine Network messaging around me. As I sped home on my one-seater hoverbike, I was distracted as a personalized holographic billboard keyed to my iCom advised, "Jane, please drive carefully." As I arrived, a Goliath iCom message reminded me to start getting ready for bed. Messaging followed me in my walls from kitchen to living room to bathroom.

As I spoke commands to my food replicator, I realized I was surrounded by wired appliances with microphones. Private space laws should protect me at home, for now. But there is no way for me to test that assumption.

Maybe Goliath already knew. How could it not? I had to stop thinking about it. Watch something distracting. Relax.

Those of us with low social merit scores are required to view more front-loaded announcements and advertisements, like the 15-minute infomercial on iCom brain implants playing in the background while I prepped dinner. *War Zone Review* was on—the SportsCenter for the forever war. As the war dragged on, and the public grew disinterested, Goliath began treating it as a sporting event to increase ratings. We bet on territory and casualty spreads. The after-battle pundits gleefully went over movie war footage and made predictions for upcoming battles.

I drew a line at trivializing a war my brother and friends were sent to die for. I turned the viewer off. My screen savers cycled through trending Network messaging: "Goliath is with you," "Support our troops, support Goliath," and simply "Go Goliath."

I sat in the near darkness, eating my crappy low-social-merit food and wondering how I would make my case with no independent media, political power, or business entity to amplify a competing message. I wished Gloria were here to hack into their communications. I now realize my concern that people wouldn't believe me or wouldn't care was misplaced. In a world where everyone's voice is preemptively silenced, they'll never even hear me.

I maintain my spirits by reading and rereading those stolen books Brian gave me. The Moon Is Down, by John Steinbeck, is about resistance to the Nazis. It is my favorite because I imagine Brian meant to compare us to the resistance, to tell me there are more oldbook adherents out there. I admit such elaborate messaging from a guy rushing to throw a box of books together is probably wishful thinking.

The hand-written card tucked inside the book offered a more tangible, if cryptic, message:

520 Chestnut Street. First Wednesdays, 8 PM. Leave <u>ALL</u> tech in hover. Down staircase by entrance 2B. Storage room. Tell no one.

What was Brian the librarian up to? I looked it up. It is an old concert hall in Seattle that has free jazz concerts on Wednesdays at 8 PM. It was unlikely such a half-forgotten prewar structure would be wired. The storage room? Surely not.

I wonder if a vast network of book preservers and Goliath doubters await me in the storage room. I fantasize about being a matriarch to a room of young rebel admirers who will recognize the game-changing potential of my investigation and enlist in it. I've gone so far as to give them names, backstories, and personalities.

I desperately want to go but keep finding reasons not to. It's an expensive trip and a day of leave. But at the core, I'm afraid it's a trap. An elaborate setup to catch me red-handed. Until I summon the courage to go, I'll keep reimagining the storage room—my new happy place. It exists only in my mind for now, and the pages of this journal.

July 3

I dreamt the police searched my apartment, found the journal, and put me on trial. No one came to defend me. Not my mother, my sister, my friends. It felt real, more premonition than nightmare. Either way, I know what caused it: creeping fear that private space laws will be stripped away. Sooner or later, my safe room will go poof.

Even worse, I worry iCom brain implants may become mandatory after supply catches up with demand for the long back-ordered tech. Then I wouldn't even have to *do* things that would cost me social merit points, just *think* them. A complete Network lobotomy.

Whatever the timing, I won't be able to hide who I am forever. They will find my dissent. They will come for me. If I'm to turn people against Goliath, if I'm to start a revolution, I need to be quick about it.

I woke from my nightmare to the purgatory of a conflicted life. My convictions shackle me. They keep me from an easier, unconflicted life. I want to remain true to them as much as I want free of them.

I nearly destroyed this journal today. I dangled its dry, handwritten pages over my stove's flames. Untethered from the Network and without backups, I could erase the handwritten evidence of my resistance and be done with it.

I calmed myself for the moment—unable to burn this journal I have so recently begun, unwilling to walk away from my obligation to the truth, to my brother, to myself. But self-preservation is a powerful instinct. My resilience buckles under an increasingly dubious risk/reward calculation.

The truth won't help David, alive or dead. It won't help anyone else, least of all me. There is no payoff for this sacrifice—a truth coalescing in my mind that I cannot dismiss. Ironically, it is my very reverence for truth that exposes the futility of my fidelity to it.

I thought exposing the war as the mother-of-all-lies would trigger outrage, an emotion we are numb to after so many years of applying it exclusively to the trivial. But our people expect to be lied to. They might even resent me for uncovering a truth that threatens our comfortable national narratives of prosperity and security.

Whether by Network design or accident, personal and political identities have merged completely. A threat to the system is a threat to the self—a brilliant failsafe to prevent revolution. At a minimum, accepting such a grand deception would require enough introspection to admit they were fooled. Unlikely.

Regardless, such a high-minded appeal to people's better angels won't happen in a vacuum. It would require sacrifice, an increasingly alien concept. We are kept fat and happy these days. Gloria used to say, "Collaboration beats rebellion every time, if the candy is good enough."

Not every time, my dear friend. Not you. But the Glorias of the world are few and far between these days. To expect the people to care beyond their narrow self-interest may be too much to ask.

Maybe they would have cared about my revelations years ago, before Goliath so conditioned us to reject old values and accept Network truth so completely. Maybe they would still, but I am no longer certain I care to pay the price for such vague hopes. All my years of screaming in the wilderness with nothing to show for it and nothing coming. Fuck the wilderness.

I keep Brian's invitation taped to this journal. I like to think I'll accept it when the time is right. But I fear it will never be right.

I take small comfort in knowing I'm not completely alone. I see skepticism growing in the youth, like Lily and Brian. But is it true conviction or just rebellious boredom? I fear their enthusiasm will wane with adulthood, as they see the rewards the Network withholds from heretics. I am not immune, so how can I expect them to be? Another small comfort that grows ever smaller.

July 4

I can't do this anymore. I'm done.

I'll hike out to my hiding spot tomorrow, but not to dig up the evidence. I'm burying this journal with it. I'm letting it go.

I don't know what I was thinking. I imagined I'd build up a case so convincing that it would compel change, maybe even convince our hidden leadership to change course. If I could not push back or was too afraid to, I imagined someone in the future coming across the journal to take up the fight. A dormant dream in the back of my mind envisions some post-Goliath generation uncovering my stash and recognizing my righteousness. At the very least, someone would know I meant well.

More than anything, I wanted to know what really happened to my baby brother. I felt I owed him that.

The lies about his death awakened me to the locust swarm of little lies the Network used to slowly obscure us from ourselves. Now I doubt everything. All my righteous anger exits my body as I accept the futility of my mission and the relatively of truth.

Did Goliath lie to us, or was it an instrument through which we lied to ourselves? When most of us willingly, even enthusiastically, accepted a system that destroyed democracy, is that not the ultimate expression of the people's true will? Is that not a kind of democracy? Is that not also the truth?

Maybe I'm just rationalizing my decision. Doesn't matter.

I'm done being a martyr for a cause only I believe in. Mary's right. There's a selfishness, an arrogance, to my fight for the truth. I'm ending it.

The only real truth is that no one cares about the truth. They only care about their truth. I am finally free from an obligation to it. I will speak its name no more.

I feel much lighter now. I can finally live in the present and embrace the Network. Someday, I hope to become the profile Goliath intends me to be.

Remnants of myself still hope someone will find this journal. Part of me still wants to know what happened to my brother. Part of me feels like a traitor. That part won't allow me to destroy my evidence stash or this journal. Burying it is a coward's compromise.

If you are reading this, it is up to you what you do with it. Perhaps you are more courageous than I am. Perhaps David would have been.

Epilogue

Jane may have given up on exposing Goliath, at least for now, but she was right about David. The Sins of theSaviors series continues with the Book 1: The Culling Box, where the truth about David's death is revealed and the Veristo family continues its collision course with the Network. Will the truth liberate or condemn them?

Until then, may Goliath preserve your social merit and never deploy you to the culling box.

From the Author

Many decades ago, I was a soldier. My unit was slated for war zone deployment. I studied the causes of the conflict and our proposed involvement. I found both wanting. It weighed on me. It seeped into my dreams. Those dreams became this story.

In recent years, I happened upon my original handwritten novel. Its dark prognostications of forever wars, resource scarcity, democracy, and technology became more prescient and urgent with time. I updated it with contemporary manifestations of these anxieties, including AI, social media, and polarization.

The series begins with the election of 2028, based on trends established much earlier. This is speculative science fiction of the near future. Could it soon become our present? I want to know what you think. Let me know at: dystopiandreamspress@outlook.com.

Many thanks for reading. Please provide a review and help this book break free of the Network's logarithmic shackles.

Other Books in the Sins of the Saviors Series

Book 1: The Culling Box (2025)

Book 2: The Price of Prosperity
(Coming in 2025)

Dystopian Dreams

dystopiandreamspress@outlook.com

www.ingramcontent.com/pod-product-compliance
Lightning Source LLC
Chambersburg PA
CBHW071341130626
46556CB00004B/1972

* 9 7 9 8 9 9 2 0 4 7 1 3 4 *